UP THE CREEK

To the women in my life, Abbey and Sienna

Text and illustrations © 2013 Nicholas Oldland

Kids Can Press acknowledges the financial support of the Government of Ontario, through the Ontario Media Development Corporation's Ontario Book Initiative; the Ontario Arts Council; the Canada Council for the Arts; and the Government of Canada, through the CBF, for our publishing activity.

Published in Canada by
Kids Can Press Ltd.
25 Dockside Drive
Toronto, ON M5A 0B5

Published in the U.S. by
Kids Can Press Ltd.
2250 Military Road
Tonawanda, NY 14150

www.kidscanpress.com

The artwork in this book was rendered in Photoshop.
The text is set in Animated Gothic and Handysans.

Edited by Yvette Ghione
Designed by Marie Bartholomew and Julia Naimska

This book is smyth sewn casebound.

Manufactured in Malaysia, in 10/2013
by Tien Wah Press (Pte) Ltd.

CM 13 0 9 8 7 6 5 4 3 2

Library and Archives Canada Cataloguing in Publication

Oldland, Nicholas, 1972–
Up the creek / Nicholas Oldland.

(Life in the wild)
ISBN 978-1-894786-32-4

I. Title.   II. Series: Life in the wild.

PS8629.L46U6 2013   jC813'.6   C2013-900005-4

Kids Can Press is a *Corus*™ Entertainment company

UP THE CREEK

Nicholas Oldland

Kids Can Press

There once was a bear, a moose and a beaver who were
the best of friends, though they often disagreed.

One sunny day, the bear, the moose and the beaver decided to go canoeing.

The moose wanted to steer, but
so did the bear and the beaver.
They all sat in the stern.

With so much weight in the back of the canoe,
it tipped, and they ended up in the water.

So they played Eenie-Meenie-Minie-Moe, and it was decided that the moose would steer. They all settled back into the canoe and began to paddle.

The bear insisted on paddling portside, but the beaver and the moose also preferred the left. With everyone paddling on the same side, they traveled in circles.

Soon their arms grew tired,
so they began to switch sides. That's when
they finally started to travel in a straight line.
But just as they began to make progress, they
came to a stop at a beaver dam.

They all had different ideas as to how to get across.
The beaver wanted to push the canoe. But that didn't work.

The moose thought they should pull the canoe. That didn't work either.

Fortunately the bear figured it out. The only way across was to portage.

Back in the water, the bear, the moose and the beaver settled into a rhythm and started to really enjoy paddling along the river.

But it wasn't long before they began to argue. They argued so loudly that they didn't notice the current growing stronger or the quiet rumbling in the distance ...

Until it was too late!

The river had turned into wild white-water rapids.

Thrown sideways, underwater, through the air and everywhere, the bear, the moose and the beaver held on for their lives.

Exhausted, bruised and wet, the three friends landed on a rock in the middle of the rapids.

The moose wanted to burn the canoe
to make a signal fire.

The bear wanted to throw
the beaver to shore to get help.

The beaver figured swimming to shore would be safer.

They argued over whose plan was best well into the night.

The next morning, it dawned on the bear, the moose and the beaver that they would have to work together to make it home safely.

So they climbed back into their battered canoe,
took a deep breath and ran the rapids.

They twisted, leaped, crashed and blasted through the water.

The rapids were fierce, but
with the bear's powerful strokes,
the moose's steady hoof and
the beaver's clever commands,
they set a true, clear course.

At last, the bear, the moose and the beaver made it to shore.

After a much-needed nap, the bear, the moose and the beaver
worked together to repair their canoe and paddles ...

Catch some fish ...

And cook lunch.

Before they tucked into their meal, they all gave
thanks for the wildest adventure they had ever had.

Rested and relaxed, the bear,
the moose and the beaver were ready to set out for home.

After taking a long look at the raging rapids, they decided
to walk. And who could disagree with that?